Whitcomb Springs

A Whitcomb Springs Short Story

MK McClintock

For Samantha, Christi, and Lynn.
Thank you for being a part of this adventure.

AUTHOR'S NOTE

An Abridged History of Whitcomb Springs

FOUNDED IN 1860 by Daniel and Evelyn Whitcomb, in what was then the Nebraska Territory, the mountain town of Whitcomb Springs started with a trading post (now the general store) and two cabins. Daniel and two friends from Pennsylvania, James Bair and Charles Carroll, founded the Whitcomb Timber Company in 1860. James Bair died the first winter after arriving in Montana, caught in a blizzard unawares. When the Civil War broke out in 1861, Daniel and Charles returned east to fight for the Union, believing it their duty to their country and their home state of Pennsylvania.

Evelyn had a choice to make—return home or wait for her husband, as Daniel promised to return soon. "The war would not last more than a few months," he had said. And so she chose to remain in Whitcomb Springs. Months became years, and under Evelyn's close watch and the help of a friend, the town grew year by year. The Whitcomb Timber Company added "Mining" to its name, and it continued to prosper.

Nebraska Territory became the Montana Territory on May 26, 1864.

As families, tradesmen, and miners came to the mountain valley, Evelyn Whitcomb offered ownership in businesses to hard workers, benefiting both the town and its citizens, a number that reached one hundred and fifty souls by the end of the war.

Although the war did not extend to the Northwest Territories, the citizens of Whitcomb Springs feared for friends and family caught in the tumult. When the war ended in 1865, many who had built a life in the valley had lost and loved, prospered and hoped.

These are their stories.

Whitcomb Springs

A Short Story

Whitcomb Springs, Montana Territory
April 25, 1865

THE LETTER FLUTTERED to the table. Evelyn stared at the sheet of paper but could no longer make out the words as they blurred together. *Surrender.* She prayed this day would come, they all had, and after four tortuous years, the war was finally over.

There would be more capitulation on the part of the South, and too many families who would never see their men again . . . but it was over.

Separated, yet not untouched, from conflict, Evelyn Whitcomb lived in the same town her husband and their two friends founded one year before news of the Civil War reached them. By way of her sister, who lived in Rose Valley, Pennsylvania with their parents, they were kept informed as often as Abigail could get a letter through. Evelyn often wondered if she should have returned to Rose Valley to help with the war effort, much as her sister Abigail had done, yet she found the needs of Whitcomb Springs to be vast as the town continued to grow.

Many men and boys left, leaving their wives, mothers, and sisters behind to fight for a cause they didn't fully understand, yet still felt it their duty to serve. Others remained behind to continue working in the mine and watch over those families with or without kin.

Evelyn read over Abigail's letter once more, letting the words settle into her mind, for even now she struggled to believe it was over—that her husband might return home.

Dearest Evelyn,

For too many years now I have shared with you the horrors and travesties befallen many of the young men with whom we spent our childhood. News has reached us that on the ninth of April, Robert E. Lee surrendered to Ulysses S. Grant at Appomattox Courthouse. Oh, sister, I dared not believe it was true when Papa brought home the news. He tells us not to become overly excited for there will surely be a few more battles waged until the news reaches both sides, but we can thank God that this war is officially over.

Your news of Daniel's disappearance has weighed heavy on my mind these past months since we heard, and Papa has attempted to learn of his whereabouts, to no avail. We have not given up! There is much confusion right now on both sides and Papa said it could be weeks or months more before the men return home. Do not lose faith, sweet Evie.

Your most loving sister,
Abigail

Evelyn pressed her face against her open handkerchief and wept against the cloth. The letter lay open on the table where it landed, for the moment forgotten. She did not have to witness smoke rising from destructed battlefields or watch neighbors' homes burn to ash like they did in the battle-worn regions back east, but Whitcomb Springs had not been spared from the emotional onslaught. Three husbands and two young sons had been sent home to be buried, including Charles Carroll, one of their partners in the founding of the town and mine. She wrote to Daniel when news of Charles's death reached his widow and young daughter, but Daniel did not respond for months, and even then it did not sound as though her letter about Charles's death found him.

He spoke of his love for her and of life after the war. They'd moved away from Pennsylvania five years prior, but he and Charles had still considered it their duty to fight. Friends since childhood, they did everything together, and going to war was no exception.

Evelyn slammed her fist on the letter and freed four years' worth of accumulated anger into her tears. As the town matriarch, even at her young age, Evelyn taught geography and history at the school, worked alongside the townspeople to establish a community garden, and offered whatever comfort she could to the wives and children whose men were lost or still away. She filled four years of days with enough activity to keep her too busy to feel the weight of the lonely nights. Alone now in the quiet of her parlor with her sister's letter dotted in tears, Evelyn relinquished herself to grief and the flood of memories from a happier time.

Nebraska Territory
June 15, 1860

"I WANTED ADVENTURE, Daniel, but I do believe you've gone too far this time." Evelyn dabbed her handkerchief against her neck. The air, still cool on the early summer day, warmed by degrees the farther they rode. It was her first time riding a horse outside a manicured park or gently sloping pasture, and the rough terrain proved to be more difficult than she'd originally credited.

Their guide, who went only by the name of Cooper, promised them what they'd see at the end of the trail would be worth the two days' ride to get there. Evelyn had seen beautiful scenery, but nothing so far as to make her trust the man whose appearance was as untamed as the trail on which they now traveled.

"We're almost there, Evie," Daniel said. He urged his horse forward so he rode beside his wife. "Didn't I tell you the West was spectacular?"

"Yes, you did." They were blessed with so much and yet they'd lost what was most important to them. Two children—sons—passed away shortly after their births, one year apart. They suffered together, mourned together, and dreamed together of a life far removed from their sorrows. He promised her adventure in a place grander than anything she'd ever seen. His promises were based on stories and reports of western expansion, and she loved him enough to believe in his dream as much as he did.

After weeks of train travel, cramped stage coaches,

and a few months' extended stay in Helena, Evelyn had endured enough dreaming. "Daniel, please tell our guide we must stop and rest."

Daniel pulled his horse to a stop, called out to Cooper, and helped Evelyn down from the saddle. The muscles in her back and legs were of little help to hold her upright. Daniel kept her steady, and she leaned toward him. He stood half a foot taller than her five and a half feet. Never one to be considered strong, he was lean and in excellent health from years of horse riding and exploring the Pennsylvania hills. When he asked if she wanted to remain in Helena while he joined the scout, she'd been quick to assure him she could handle the journey.

Four days of stage, wagon, and horseback, and she'd kept her silence until now. As though sensing she didn't want to get back on the horse, Daniel positioned an arm at her waist and told their scout they were going for a walk.

Cooper lifted the saddle off his horse and moved to do the same on the others. "Be sure you stick to the trail and don't go so far I can't hear you shout."

Evelyn glanced back at Cooper, wondering what event would require them to shout, and thought better of asking. She walked alongside her husband, staying on the trail as told. A steady rushing creek followed the trail as it widened, then narrowed. When they turned a bend around a copse of pine trees thick with branches and lush green needles, Evelyn stopped.

"Daniel." Her voice was a reverent whisper. She dropped his hand and stepped forward, her eyes moving back and forth over the landscape so as not to miss anything.

"I promised you, Evie." Daniel stood behind her and wrapped his arms around her waist. They were home.

Whitcomb Springs, Montana Territory
April 25, 1865

THE PIONEER MOUNTAINS, still capped with snow, rose above the hills surrounding their valley and the town. Breathtaking had been the first word uttered from her lips when she and Daniel stood at the edge of the valley. Evelyn picked up where her husband left off, and together they succeeded in building the town Daniel dreamt of, a town that would prosper without destroying the land.

The road was made passable their first summer, with a lot of expense, time, and hard labor of strong men hired to help build the first cabins and a trading post. Daniel promised he would build her a grand house, and it was the last thing he finished before he left.

The trading post was now a general store. Homes and businesses lined the carefully mapped roads, and last year they finished the church. Evelyn wondered what Daniel would say about the town when he returned. Pleased and proud, she hoped.

A gentle yet insistent knock at her front door drew her slowly from her own worries. Though more than two weeks had passed since the surrender, some would have heard the news and shared it with others until the whole town new. They did not have a telegraph or a post office yet, and letters from the East did not always reach them quickly. Townsfolk had families in the North and others in the South, yet here in Whitcomb Springs, they took no sides in the conflict of politics of war.

Evelyn blotted the tears away, took a few deep breaths, and rose from the chair. She wavered and kept herself upright by leaning on the table. Once her legs stopped trembling, she walked through the hall into the foyer. The knocking ceased, but a face pressed against the glass in the window, a cherub's face with red cheeks and wide brown eyes, surrounded by a halo of wispy blond hair.

The young girl waved and stepped back when

Evelyn opened the door. "Missouri Woodward, you appear to have been in a spot of trouble." She looked over the girl's dusty dress, muddy boots, and a shawl covered in leaves.

Missouri grinned. "Monroe said girls couldn't climb trees because we're too puny."

"And you proved him wrong."

The six-year-old bobbed her head and straightened her shawl. "Mama won't be mad when I tell her. She says girls are just as cap . . ."

"Capable," Evelyn said while holding back a grin of her own.

"That's it. Mama says girls can do anything they want."

Evelyn believed Missouri's mother, a learned woman from Charleston and supporter of Elizabeth Cady Stanton, a leading figure of the women's rights movement, would teach her daughter to stand up for herself, but she also knew Lydia Woodward to be a lady of impeccable taste and manners. Evelyn held the door open and invited Missouri inside. "Your mother will understand, but even so, let's clean you up a little before you go home, and you can tell me what brought you to my door this morning."

Evelyn helped Missouri clean off her leather boots and remove the leaves and twigs from the shawl. She managed to wipe away some of the dust from the dress, but evidence of her shenanigans remained. From one of the few families in town of old money, Lydia Woodward had remained in Whitcomb Springs with her two children—Missouri and her older brother, Monroe—after her husband returned to Charleston to fight for the Southern cause. Lydia may have supported the beliefs of Elizabeth Stanton and feminist reformers, but she avoided the topic of reform when around Evelyn.

Women's rights were inevitable, this she believed, yet to speak of such things while her husband and so many other men and boys were at war somehow seemed disloyal to their sacrifices. From an established and wealthy family in Pennsylvania herself, Evelyn had everything she ever wanted, and her father encouraged an education beyond needlework and home management for his daughters. The stifling existence women like Lydia spoke of was foreign to Evelyn.

Even now, thousands of miles from home, she had both money and property. And she would give up both if only to have her husband back in her arms, to wake in the morning with him beside her, and to know he was safe—to know they would grow old together. She smoothed out Missouri's skirts and declared the girl fit enough to return home.

"Wait, Missouri. What brought you here, besides your dusty clothes?"

"Mama said Papa is coming home soon. Since you know everything and I guessed maybe if you said he was really coming home, it would be true."

Evelyn leaned back in the chair at the kitchen table and studied the girl. Hope, a useful commodity in the hands of the right person. Missouri Woodward possessed it in abundance. How to speak the truth without quashing hope? Evelyn wondered. If there was one way to quickly spread news of the surrender to those who had yet to hear, it was Missouri. "What has your mother told you about where your father has been these past years?"

"Protecting South Carolina. It's where I was born, and Mama said her mama and papa live there, but I don't get to see them anymore. I want to see them, but Mama said when Papa comes home we can go for a visit, so I really want Papa to come home."

It was not her place to explain the war to someone else's child, or to reveal the realities of life and death, so Evelyn chose her next words carefully. "Your father and many other fathers and brothers and sons are protecting their homes, but what caused them to fight is over now."

"Does that mean they're coming home?"

"Some of them will, and others won't."

The big brown eyes looked up at Evelyn. "You mean like when Mary's papa came back, and we all went to the cemetery?"

Evelyn lowered herself to the girl's level and squeezed Missouri's hands. "We don't know what comes next. However, we need to be strong for each other, no matter what. And you have so much hope in you; hold onto it."

Missouri nodded and fell against Evelyn. Her eyes remained dry, yet she held herself close for a few minutes before leaning back. "Sally Benson said my papa might not come home. Her mama is taking them back to . . ."

"Georgia."

"That's right."

Evelyn kept her sigh silent in the face of frustration. She'd heard of the Benson's decision to return to their native Georgia a few days ago. They were one of the families where husband and father had died, but there was no body left to send home.

"Missouri, I want you to promise me something."

"All right, Mrs. Whitcomb."

"No matter what you hear or what others say, remember to listen to your heart. Be strong and brave and never let anyone tell you your hopes are impossible."

"I don't understand, Mrs. Whitcomb."

Evelyn kissed the girl's cheek and said, "You will. Now run along to your mother. She'll wonder where you've gone."

With a quiet "thank you" and another quick hug, Missouri exited the house. Evelyn watched her run down the front walk and pass the beds of flowers eager to sprout and bloom before she remembered to slow down. One day soon, Evelyn thought, young girls will run and jump and play in the dirt without worrying if their fathers or brothers were coming back to them.

She stood on her wide front porch of the beautiful home Daniel had built, nestled in the untouched Montana valley. After four years of living without her husband, not knowing if he'd return to her, Evelyn still sought comfort from standing on the porch and looking up at the towering peaks. A few townspeople turned soil, preparing the community garden for seeds. Everyone who lived in town spent a few hours a week taking turns in the garden, and everyone reaped the benefits.

The community had been her family these long years, and she knew how blessed she was to want for nothing while others struggled. The garden had been a way to fill a need. She supplied the tools and seeds and looked forward to her turn to tend to the beds. The simple task of planting and watching the vegetables and flowers grow was a rewarding task.

She hired two of the young widows, Harriet Barker and Tabitha Armstrong, to help with her personal gardens and tend the house. Both women lived in rooms on the second floor, rooms that remained vacant and too quiet after Daniel left.

"Mrs. Whitcomb!" Lilian Cosgrove, who lived with her wounded husband in a small cottage on the other side of the meadow, hurried up the walkway. "Evelyn, please come quickly to the church."

Evelyn darted a glance down the road, but didn't see or hear a reason for Lilian to look flushed or to carry the heavy burden of worry in her eyes.

"Lilian, what's happened?"

Lilian darted a glance to the family across the way in the garden and lowered her voice. "There's something you need to see in the church. Ever since Reverend Mitchum left to tend that orphanage in San Francisco, Jedediah has been keeping a watch on the church, as you know. Today he found . . . oh, please come."

Bemused, though not surprised as Lilian had a tendency toward melodrama, Evelyn followed the woman down the street, past the small hotel, and into the meadow where the church stood. Daniel and Evelyn always meant for it to be a place of solace for anyone who stepped through its doors. It wasn't uncommon to find people passing through town, spending a few minutes inside before they moved on.

"Lilian, what is going on?" Evelyn stepped into the dimly lit building. The gray skies outside blocked much of the natural sunlight the row of windows often let into the church.

"You'll see, in the back."

Evelyn followed her friend to the back room where the reverend once lived. Sitting around the scarred table was a man, a woman, and a young boy, who looked no more than four years old, nestled on his mother's lap. Jedediah Cosgrove stood in front of the only exit.

The man at the table started to stand but quickly took his seat again. Evelyn moved her eyes to look at the man's legs. One appeared to be confined in a wooden leg brace. "Please, there's no need to stand." She took in the frightened expressions of the mother and child and looked at the others. "What's going on, Jedediah?"

"Jed saw her stealing from our garden," Lilian said. "He followed her here and found them living in these rooms."

Disappointment flooded through Evelyn's heart. She would speak with her friends later, but now, the couple and their children needed tending.

"There is no reason to be afraid. What are your names?"

The man again attempted to stand, but his wife pressed him down with a gentle touch and passed him their son. "Corbel. I'm Olive and my husband, Levi. This is our son, Elijah. We didn't mean any harm."

Evelyn was quick to reassure her. "I'm sure you didn't. I see you're injured, Mr. Corbel."

Olive spoke instead of Levi. "My husband doesn't speak, ma'am, not since . . ." she looked at her man, ". . . since he came home."

"I'm Evelyn Whitcomb." Evelyn turned to Lilian and Jed. "Thank you, Lilian, and Jed, it's okay. Please leave us. I'd like to speak with the Corbels."

"Are you sure it's safe?" Lilian asked.

Evelyn fought back the sadness at her friend's words. "Yes, I'm sure. I would like to visit with the Corbels alone for a few minutes. I'll come see you afterward." She rarely used her place in the community as a voice of authority, but when she did, those around her offered no argument. Evelyn waited until she heard the front doors of the church close.

When she faced the family again, Olive was still

standing. "May I sit with you?"

Surprise replaced wariness and Olive nodded. Once Evelyn sat in the only empty chair, Olive followed suit. Evelyn said, "I'm sorry for my friends' behavior. They're protective when it comes to strangers."

"I shouldn't have stolen from them." Olive lifted her son back onto her lap. "We were traveling and sorry to say, we found ourselves off the trail."

"That's not difficult to do up here." Evelyn studied each of them, the gaunt faces and mended clothes. They were clean, indicating Olive's close care of her family. "Does the leg pain you, Mr. Corbel?"

He shook his head. "I can take it, ma'am." She barely caught his words. The hoarse whisper lost what little volume it had between them.

Evelyn cast a surprised look in Olive's direction. Olive explained, "I didn't tell you a falsehood, Mrs. Whitcomb. It's easier, you see, for people to think . . . Levi was scarred something fierce, and it pains him to speak."

"I am not accusing you of misleading me, not at all. How was he injured, if it's not too impertinent to ask?"

Olive and her husband exchanged a silent look, and he nodded once. Olive said, "He fought for the Confederacy. There was an explosion, but Levi prefers not to talk about it, ma'am. Not the explosion or the war."

"Please, call me Evelyn. And it's all right, I shouldn't have pried. Please accept my apologies. My husband hasn't returned home, and I don't know if he will, so I do understand a bit of what your family has suffered. Where are you going, if I may ask?"

"We're from Texas. When Levi was . . . after he returned, we lost our farm. We came north, heard there were opportunities up here, been finding work where we can." Olive sat higher in the chair, her back straightening as she held her son closer. "Are you going to turn us over to your sheriff?"

"As it happens, we don't have a sheriff right now."

"But we saw—"

"A sheriff's office, yes. We're a growing town and like to plan for the future."

"We saw a sign when we came into town: Whitcomb Springs. Is that you?"

Evelyn nodded. "My husband is Daniel Whitcomb. This town was our dream." Evelyn stood. "It's a place for new beginnings, if that's what you're after."

All three pairs of eyes met hers. Levi said in his whispered words, "Mrs. Whitcomb?" Those two words asked far more than a confirmation of her name. She couldn't help Daniel except with prayers, and right now she believed these people needed her attention more.

"These rooms are yours to use while you decide what to do next. There's a well out back and I'll have clean linens, food, and changes of clothes brought over. If you choose to leave, at least you will be rested. If you choose to stay, we will find a place for you and discuss your options."

"I don't understand, Mrs.—Evelyn."

"It's our way, Mrs. Corbel. There's work for those who are willing to work hard and there's a home here for those in search of one. Life in Whitcomb Springs is not always easy. It's rewarding, and the community is strong, and most importantly, it's ours." Evelyn saw from the way they looked at her that she'd given them enough to think about. "I'll send someone along with the items I mentioned. If you'd like to visit again, my house is down the north road past the general store. I would like to help if you'll let me."

Evelyn left them to their privacy. She didn't know if she'd see them again or if in the night they planned to disappear in hopes of reaching a new destination. Either way, there was another matter to tend, one she dreaded.

Lilian and Jed weren't waiting outside. She walked to the edge of the meadow and crossed the bridge over a narrow point of Little Bear Creek. They stepped outside when she approached.

"Have then gone?" Lilian asked.

"They are welcome here, Lilian, as you and Jed were five years past."

"They stole from us."

Evelyn's heart ached at the other woman's harsh words. "True, and I suspect they will repay you in any way they can. Where is your charity, Lilian, and yours, Jed? You were injured and by grace you came home to your wife. Others have suffered far more. Olive had a son to feed and only a mother's desperation would have had her committing a crime, but it is a minor one. She stole food from your garden to feed her son, food that can be replaced. They are to be forgiven."

Jed stepped forward, chagrined. "I'm sorry, Mrs. Whitcomb. You're right. I don't reckon I know what would have become of Lilian and me if we hadn't found this town, or if I hadn't come back to her."

"I appreciate—"

"But I ain't never stolen."

"I see." And Evelyn did.

Lilian held a white cloth in one hand and her other still showed evidence of flour from baking. "This town isn't for people like them. We've worked too hard."

Evelyn fought back tears for the loss of two people she'd called friends—family, even. "I know well enough what kind of people belong in this town. People like the Corbels. These mountains that surround us, the valley where we build our homes and grow our crops, don't belong to us. We put our name on a sign and erected this town. We burrowed into the earth so the mine could support the town and the people in it, and when we're done, we do everything we can to make the land whole again. We don't take what we don't need, and we give what we can. That has always been Whitcomb Springs." Evelyn walked away, stopped after a few feet and looked back at them. "At what point did you forget?"

EVELYN WIPED THE back of her sleeve over her damp brow. The spring morning brought with it rare sunshine and a sky as blue as the wild flax sprouting in the meadows. An early rain softened the soil, allowing her cultivator to move effortlessly through the rich, brown earth. She relished the hour she spent every morning in her flower beds before she took a turn at the community garden.

Harriett cut a spade into the dirt a few beds away, leaving Evelyn to enjoy the quiet of her own thoughts. One of the kitchen windows was open to let in the cool air and out wafted the scent of Tabitha's culinary talents. There would be fresh baked bread and a sweet pastry of some sort to sell in the general store. Evelyn would see to it that the Corbels received a healthy ration of bread, baby vegetables from the garden, meat from Evelyn's personal stores, and of course something sweet for young Peter.

A maze of old roots latched onto the hand tool, and with expert skill, Evelyn searched the ground until her fingers touched a bulb. She brought it closer to the surface and recovered it before moving onto the next section. Evelyn much preferred gardening to kitchen work. She learned what was needed to so she and Daniel wouldn't starve during those early days in their new home. Tabitha lost her husband in a hunting accident soon after they moved to Whitcomb Springs, and though the circumstances came with sadness, Evelyn thanked the Lord every day for Tabitha.

Harriett's husband made her a widow six months after they married on her twentieth birthday. After a year under Evelyn's roof, the young woman had yet to share how her husband died. Whispers among the townspeople about what might have happened dispelled when Evelyn stood up and vouched for Harriett. These women were as much her sisters as the one she left behind in Pennsylvania.

She sat back on her heels and straightened the stiffness from her body. A twinge in her lower back told her she'd been working longer than planned. She removed one of her leather gloves, long ago ruined for anything except manual labor, and pulled Daniel's watch from her apron pocket. A gift from his father when they had left home to come west, Daniel had asked her to keep it close while he was gone, to remind her he would return. Evelyn kept it polished and with her, always. The face indicated nine o'clock, and she tucked the gold watch and chain back into her pocket.

She looked at the expansive community garden next to hers. It had started out as a way to serve her, Daniel, James, and Charles, but as others came to help build the town—and stay—Evelyn saw a new need arise. Many families had small gardens to feed their own, but many contributed to and enjoyed the bounty from the town's garden. The Wiley family would arrive in another hour for their turn.

They had a few weeks yet before most of the vegetables sprouted, and longer still until many of them were ready to harvest. In the meantime, most families, herself included, subsisted off canned vegetables and fruits. A small greenhouse, finished last summer, provided fresh vegetables throughout the year, rationed, of course.

Evelyn remembered the Shelton Estate Greenhouses her family once visited in Massachusetts.

Impressive in their scale and variety of plants within, they sparked an idea in Evelyn that took root. She had received skepticism when she'd explained to Cooper what she wanted built on the land near her home. Close enough to access when the weather turned inclement, yet far enough away for the house not to block the sunlight. Wasted expense, Cooper had told her, and impossible to get someone to haul the supplies she needed. Evelyn ignored him and endured the murmurs from the townspeople, even as she paid dearly for materials and labor. When the structure was complete, raised beds built inside, and the first seeds planted, doubt turned to gratitude.

No one in town knew the extent of her family's wealth, not even Cooper. She'd heard stories of the eccentric Whitcomb woman who decided to build a town on her own in the remote mountain valley of Montana. No one seemed to remember Daniel or that without him, she never would have ventured this far. Or would she have? Evelyn sometimes wondered if she longed for adventure because it's what she wanted or because Daniel's thirst for it was contagious. Either way, she'd found her place and people who needed her.

Harriett stepped between Evelyn and the morning sun, casting a shadow that made it possible for Evelyn to tilt her head back without squinting. Harriett, with a spade in hand and dirt on her apron, said, "Are you all right, Evelyn? You look as though you took to wandering in your mind for a spell."

Evelyn smiled, braced a hand on the fence, and pushed up to her feet, much like a toddler does when they're learning to stand. She'd been on the ground without respite for almost two hours. "I suppose I was." She shifted her eyes to look over the area where Harriett had been working. "The gardens get lovelier every year. The soil is rich, and we had a good winter. If the rain and sun continue to share the sky these next months, we can expect a good crop from the community garden."

"More food will be a blessing. Purdy Lutts got a letter yesterday from her kin in Missouri. Her son is gone now, too, and just a few months after her husband."

News, gossip, and sickness moved quickly through a town the size of Whitcomb Springs. The only people who wouldn't know about Purdy Lutts's recent loss lived on more isolated farms and small ranches outside town. Soon enough, they would all come into town to order or pick up supplies, and when they left again, it would be with full wagons and the latest happenings.

Harriett continued. "And Betty Miles had a letter from her husband, too. He's lost an arm and won't be able to work out here. He's sent for her. She doesn't want to live in Florida with his folks, but she's got no choice."

"Harriett, how do you always hear of these things before everyone else?"

"I make sure I'm working in the general store when the supply wagon comes through."

Daniel had negotiated with a driver in Butte to deliver supplies once a month to their fledgling homestead. It took buying the man a new wagon and a healthy pair of strong mules before he agreed. Most supplies took weeks or months to arrive as there was yet no train into Montana. The trips to Whitcomb Springs turned out to be a profitable venture for the driver since he stopped at two other small communities when making the trip. As the town slowly grew, once a month turned into twice. The mail came through on the same wagon, which meant most folks getting a letter received news on the same days as everyone else.

Exceptions were made, of course. The worst of news traveled faster, if whoever sending the news could afford a private courier, but that was rare. Evelyn had received a few such letters from her family, as did other families of means in the town, but most had to wait and worry.

Evelyn gathered her tools and dropped them in a

basket along with the pulled weeds. "I am sorry to hear about Betty's eminent departure. I'll pay her a visit today, and one to Purdy as well."

"I don't know what Purdy will do with both her son and husband gone. She and that little girl don't have much."

Harriett had left home without an education beyond basic reading and numbers. Evelyn and Daniel brought with them a small library of books, and Evelyn saw to it that Harriett read a little every day. She'd also tutored her in etiquette, but there were still times when the young woman's early lack of education showed through, as in this case, where she spoke abruptly without checking to see if others were about. Tabitha stood in the kitchen doorway behind Harriett. At least it had only been Tabitha and not someone else from town. They had an unspoken agreement in the house that whatever was said among them stayed there. News trickled down the dirt roads quickly enough without them helping it along.

Tabitha stepped on the grass and crossed to where they stood. "Purdy lost her son?"

Harriett looked up at Tabitha, who stood a few inches taller. "Oh." She glanced all around to find they were alone. "I shouldn't have said anything out here."

Evelyn brushed off her apron and picked up her

basket. "No matter now. Word will reach everyone soon enough. Let's clean up and then I want to sample whatever heavenly treat Tabitha has whipped up in the kitchen."

The three women walked back into the house, but on the porch, Evelyn stopped and turned to look up at her mountains. Dark gray clouds hovered over a few peaks, and soon they would overtake the sun for control of the sky. A breeze picked up and forced the trees and low grass beyond the fence to sway. Evelyn sensed a shift in the air, and she wished she knew whether it was the atmosphere or an omen of dark things to come.

EVELYN SET HERSELF to the difficult task of consoling her friend, except when she arrived at the small cabin a half mile east of town, Evelyn met with a surprise. Purdy's disposition was not that of a woman who only yesterday heard of her son's death. She smiled in greeting when Evelyn walked up carrying two baskets, one she would leave with Purdy and the other she'd take to the Corbels.

"Hello Evelyn!" Purdy unhooked the last dry sheet from the clothesline and lifted the basket of clean linens. "I hope you'll join me for an early tea. I have plenty to spare." Like a prairie wind, Purdy hurried indoors without a wasted step. She continued talking about the weather, the progress of the mine, and the new baby born last week. She mentioned nothing of the letter or her son.

She left Evelyn to follow her inside and motioned for her to have a seat while she put away the wash. Purdy moved through the motions of placing tea and fresh scones on the table. Evelyn didn't mention it was hours before teatime or that Purdy rarely baked since her husband and son went to war.

"Won't you sit and join me, Purdy?"

Purdy stopped and looked at Evelyn. Her eyes stared at Evelyn with a blank expression for several seconds before her hands started to shake. She shook her head and returned to kitchen work. "I can't stop. Not for a minute, for a second. I can't stop."

Evelyn rose from the chair and reached for Purdy. The other woman's body tightened when she stepped back a foot. She raised tear-filled eyes to Evelyn. "I can't stop. If I stop, it's real." Evelyn's arms went around Purdy's shaking body. Tears trickled down her cheeks and sobs tore from her lips. A few minutes into the uncontrolled release of grief, Evelyn saw the terrified face of a young girl peek around the corner into the kitchen. A few soft tears fell from the young girl's eyes before she moved out of sight.

An hour later, Evelyn walked away from the cabin. Tabitha had arrived and promised to watch over Purdy for the remainder of the day. No doubt others would stop into visit, either to offer condolences or hear the news firsthand about the latest young man who would not be returning to Whitcomb Springs.

Evelyn walked down the main road through the center of the small town. They'd made great progress in four years, from essential businesses to new homes. The hotel, an extravagance for their town, remained empty most of the time, but she held hope that one day the beauty of the mountains would attract visitors looking for a quiet respite and restorative holiday. Cooper still acted as a guide, bringing the occasional visitor or surveyor through. They often spent a few evenings in town before moving on. Last year a photographer came through to capture images so he could put them on display in St. Louis. Yes, she had dreams for Whitcomb Springs, but above all, she dreamed of keeping the town a safe place for those who lived and worked there.

A loud rumble brought her to a halt outside the general store. She noticed a few others also stopped what they were doing to investigate the noise. Another rumble, this time joined by a distant sound of thunder. They all looked up. Other than the dark clouds Evelyn saw earlier, the sky was clear.

Shouts not understood but far enough away to be heard repeated in a chain reaction that traveled from one person to the next until they reached her. A tree snapped. Ropes broke. Avalanche. Evelyn caught enough snippets to know a terrible accident had happened in the logging camp. She left the basket for the Corbels on the general store porch and hurried down the road. She stopped at the blacksmiths to borrow a horse from Dominik Andris.

He already had one saddled for himself. He quickly saddled a mare, helped Evelyn on the horse, and together they followed others who made their way north of town. Cooper caught up with them before they veered onto the timber trail. Three miles up the mountainside, on a narrow stretch of open land, the original logging camp sat empty. Evelyn urged her horse forward, but Cooper grabbed the reins and shook his head. "You go up there right now, they'll worry more about you than getting everyone out alive."

Since the day Cooper McCord led her and Daniel to the valley they now called home, he'd always been straight with her, even if she disliked what he had to say. Their relationship was unique; they were the truest of friends. Had she not been married . . . Evelyn didn't want to think about the possibility. She trusted

Cooper, and when it came to life and death situations, she listened. "You're going up there?"

Cooper nodded. "Dominik and I will ride up and see what's happened. Don't go up there, Evelyn."

It was the first time he'd called her Evelyn in front of others. "I won't. Please be careful, both of you."

She dismounted and tethered her horse to one of the posts in front of the foreman's cabin, the closest structure to where she stood.

Half the number of men from the town remained at home rather than fight in a war they didn't understand at the time. Some refused to leave their families behind while others didn't believe in taking up arms. Evelyn had made the decision to keep both the timber operation and the mine going these four years for the sake of the town and the families who relied on steady wages. She visited once a month, much to the concern of Cooper who always accompanied her. He worried not about the men who lived in Whitcomb Springs but the few who hired on during busier seasons, men who were passing through looking for temporary work—men who couldn't be trusted.

The man they carried down on a makeshift stretcher was no stranger passing through. She recognized him as Tabitha's older brother, William Lee, who lived and worked at the logging camp six months of the year and spent the other six months in Wyoming. He came to Whitcomb Springs after Tabitha's husband had died, and though Evelyn knew him only in passing or for the occasional meal he took at the house, he was family.

They eased the stretcher to the ground, not far from the foreman's cabin. Cooper knelt next to the body and held a hand over William's mouth to check his breathing. When he looked up, he searched the crowed until he found her. Evelyn knew William was gone.

EVELYN FOUND TABITHA in the kitchen. She stood at the long and tall wooden table near the wood stove, her hands covered in flour as she turned dough in a bowl. Her soft humming filled the air with a sweet and hopeful melody. Evelyn didn't recognize the song. The windows near the stove were open to let in the cool, fresh air, though Evelyn still noticed a hint of perspiration at Tabitha's brow. Two pies cooled on a small table away from the heat and a delicious scent wafted from the vicinity of the stove. Her friend had been busy and Evelyn knew kitchen work was Tabitha's solace, her greatest joy. Evelyn had given some thought recently to opening a small cafe for Tabitha to run, but selfishness had kept the idea at bay for too long.

Would Tabitha remain in Whitcomb Springs,

Evelyn wondered? She took another step into the kitchen and Tabitha looked up, her lips formed in a wide smile.

"Evelyn! You're back sooner than I expected." Tabitha glanced out the window. "Or I've been at this longer than I thought. A cake will be ready soon. It's a new recipe I thought could be used for our picnic on Sunday after church." Tabitha wiped her hands, covered the bowl of dough with a clean cloth, and brushed fallen strands of hair off her face. It was then her smile slowly faded. Her eyes widened, and she bit her lower lip. Evelyn had seen that expression on her friend only once before—when her husband died.

"Evelyn?"

She crossed the kitchen but Tabitha held up a hand to stop her from coming closer.

"I want to visit but I really need to clean up and get lunch ready for William. I promised him a special treat today." Tabitha pointed to the pies. "Apple is his favorite. I can extra apples every year so he always has pie in the early season." Her eyes filled with tears. "He's coming down the mountain so we can sit in the gardens. There aren't many blooms yet, but he loves the garden." Tabitha removed the cloth on the dough not yet risen and began to punch it down in the bowl.

"Tabitha." This time Evelyn placed her arm over

the other woman's shoulder, a gentle touch that set Tabitha back.

"No." Tabitha shook her head and pushed the bowl away, stepped closer to one of the open windows. "You can't say the words, not yet."

Evelyn stood in silence while Tabitha's breathing became more erratic and tears slid down her cheek. The front door opened and Harriett hurried into the kitchen. She looked first at Tabitha and then to Evelyn. "Is it true what they're saying about William?"

Evelyn kept her silence, for no words were needed to confirm the truth. Another man of Whitcomb Springs had perished. This time, not from war, yet Evelyn knew Tabitha's loss would be as sharp and unyielding as when she'd lost her husband.

"I knew." Tabitha's breathing calmed, and she held a hand over her heart. "When I saw you, your face . . . it was like when James died. When you told Harriett her husband was gone. The same face. The noise earlier . . . I thought it was thunder, a storm coming. I imagined sitting on the porch with afternoon tea, watching the rain . . ." She turned toward the window and leaned against the wall. "William loved summer. He told me this year he was staying in Whitcomb Springs for good, not going back to Wyoming in the winter. He wanted to raise horses here." She turned tear-filled eyes to Evelyn and Harriett. "It wasn't his time."

It wasn't any of their times, Evelyn thought. Sensing Tabitha needed space but not solitude, she remained where she stood. Harriett must have sensed something else because she approached Tabitha, draping an around her friend's shoulder. It was then Evelyn understood. Harriett had lost a husband, Evelyn had not. Harriett knew—absolutely knew—of Tabitha's suffering. This time the sadness was for the loss of a sibling, but still a penetrating loss to which Evelyn could not relate.

The snap of a rope and a tree fallen in the wrong direction sent William to his death, without time even to say goodbye to his sister. Too many never got the chance to say goodbye. Would Evelyn be one of them?

She walked quietly from the room and past the door Harriett had left open in her haste. She stood on her front porch listening to the sounds of the small town and thought of Daniel.

THREE DAYS HAD PASSED since William's death. Harriett and Evelyn stood on either side of Tabitha in front of his grave. Rich, brown earth covered the wood coffin Cooper had built, and most of the town huddled in the cemetery near the church. Set back from the road, across the meadow and near a year-round stream, a dozen graves with bodies, and more without, dotted the well-tended ground. The first body they'd buried was of James Bair, one of Daniel's childhood friends and a founder in the Whitcomb Timber Company. He perished his first winter, caught in a blizzard, leaving no wife or children behind. Charles Carroll, the third founder in the timber company, died three years into the war. His body was sent home to Pennsylvania and his wife and daughter soon followed. Evelyn was tired of burying men. No woman or child in Whitcomb Springs had passed away in those four years. Perhaps God decided to show mercy on them, Evelyn thought, or perhaps their time would come.

For the first time in four years, Evelyn experienced true doubt for the future coupled with an anguish that gripped her heart, encasing it in despair. They waited together by William's grave long after the townspeople departed. Olive and Levi Corbel, with their son Elijah, waited near a large oak outside the fenced-in cemetery. Evelyn met Olive's gaze and motioned for them to come forward. As a unit, the young family walked across the grass and stopped a few feet from the fresh grave.

"We wanted to offer our condolences," Olive said, and held out a small bunch of wild buttercups. It wasn't an easy flower to find in their valley, which meant Olive had taken care and time to search for the spring wildflower. "I lost my young brother to fever three years ago. It's a loss that stays in you deep, right here." She tapped her chest above her heart. Elijah grasped his mother's hand when she stepped back, his eyes wide with curiosity at the exchange.

Levi tried to speak, his words barely discernible. "Anything we can do?"

"There's nothing." Tabitha stared at them, the flowers in one hand and the other gripped tightly in Harriett's palm. "Thank you for these. William would have liked them."

Evelyn left Harriett to look after Tabitha while she walked toward the church with the Corbels. She didn't venture too far in case her friends needed her. No, not just friends. They were her family. The townspeople, the strangers who passed through, they were her family, too. She said to the Corbels, "It was kind of you to bring the flowers."

"I heard about the young man who died, heard it was her brother."

Evelyn nodded. "News moves quickly here. His loss will be felt for a long time to come."

Olive hesitated with her next words, but with some encouragement from her husband, she said, "Did you mean what you said about us staying on?"

"I did. We'll find a place for you, if you want to stay."

"I can work. Levi can't talk well, or ride, but he has a good mind and knows about the land. We'd like to farm again, and . . . we can't think of anyplace we'd rather go, leastways not right now."

"It so happens we could use another good farmer in Whitcomb Springs."

ANOTHER WEEK DRIFTED by, and Evelyn waited. Three men returned home to their families. Two wives received word that their husbands died in final battles: one at Appomattox and another at the Battle of West Point, a day after President Lincoln's assassination. Another woman heard from her son who said he wasn't ready to return home. Life continued forward. Evelyn dug her spade through the damp earth. Two days of heavy rain had left plants and seedlings wilted, but the sun peeked around the edge of a thick pillow of clouds pushing away the gloom. Tabitha worked nonstop in the kitchen, volunteering to teach some of the children about cooking, digging in the community garden at least twice a day, and filling in at the general store whenever she could. Evelyn and Harriet worried but said nothing. Tabitha slept and ate, relieving some of their concern, but she kept her body and mind too busy to think of her brother.

"Evelyn?"

Evelyn shifted and smiled at Olive. "Welcome, Olive. How lovely to see you." She pushed herself up from where she knelt in the dirt and brushed away a few clumps of mud. "Do you have time for tea?"

"That's kind of you, but I need to be getting back. I came to deliver these letters that arrived with the supply wagon." Olive held out three envelopes, which Evelyn accepted.

"Thank you, Olive. One of us usually picks up the mail at the store. This is a treat." Evelyn marveled at the change in Olive in the short while since she started to work two shifts a week at the general store and two more at the hotel. Gone was the gauntness and burden of fear. No longer did she need to worry about her next meal or wonder where her family would lay their heads at night.

The Corbels worked hard and went beyond earning their keep. The two acres of land that once belonged to James Bair, along with the tidy cabin, suited the family's needs. They kindly declined further help, already overwhelmed at the kindness shown to them by most of the townspeople.

Evelyn noticed Olive looking over the established

gardens. James Bair's plot of land had gone untended the past four years. Evelyn saw to it that the cabin was kept in good repair, but the land was left to nature's devices. "How is the clearing coming along?"

Olive faced her again and smiled. "A quarter acre is almost ready for planting. The Dockett boy, Timothy, has been a big help to Levi."

Evelyn heard of Timothy Dockett, a young man of sixteen years, helping the Corbels. She doubted they could pay much, even with the extra she paid Olive for her work at the general store. It was precious little extra, for the proud woman refused charity. She paid Jed and Lilian for the vegetables stolen in desperation, an action which had surprised Lilian and left Jed wondering if he'd been wrong about the newcomers. "I know Timothy is grateful for the work. He has his heart set on attending college."

"Oh he's been wonderful for Levi to have around. It will be years yet before Elijah can help with farming, and by then—"

"By then, anything can happen," Evelyn finished for her. "Will you come for tea tomorrow? If you have time."

Obviously surprised at a second invitation, Olive nodded. "I'd like that. I did want to ask . . . how is Mrs. Armstrong fairing?"

Evelyn made sure neither Tabitha nor Harriett were in hearing distance. "She's better. It takes time."

Olive nodded, asked Evelyn to give Tabitha her good wishes, and she walked back down the road. Harriett approached and said, "Folks are taking well to the Corbels. I've visited a time or two. The young one, Elijah, is a good boy." There was a wistfulness in Harriett's voice. She'd lost a child at birth, shortly before her husband passed. That loss held pain to which Evelyn could relate.

"Harriett, would you do something for me?"

"Of course."

"I want to gather a few seedlings, both vegetables and flowers, for Olive. She mentioned they'll have enough land cleared soon to start planting."

"I don't reckon she'll accept them, unless she buys them."

"I'll figure something out."

EVELYN SAT AT the desk in her parlor and read over the first letter from home. One of the letter's Olive dropped off had been from Tabitha's family. Evelyn knew Tabitha's parents lived in Oregon and hoped one day their daughter would return. Tabitha confessed once that she and her mother didn't get along too well. She faced a difficult decision, and Evelyn worried for her.

The other two letters were from Pennsylvania: one from her mother and the other from her sister. As her sister didn't sweeten the truth, whether the news was good or bad, Evelyn read her mother's letter first. She wanted to put off any potential bad news a little longer. Her mother spoke of news from their acquaintances and a few social events to celebrate the end of the war. She mentioned two young men Evelyn knew in her youth, who had not returned. She moved quickly past the sad news and recounted details of new improvements to the house and gardens. It was her mother's way of coping, and Evelyn didn't begrudge her. The letter ended with a request for her to return home now that the war had ended.

She set her mother's letter aside and opened Abigail's.

Dearest Evelyn,

I shan't wait on the most important news, which I imagine you've waited for long enough. Daniel is alive!

Evelyn gasped and released a shaky breath. Her hands shook as she continued reading.

Papa doesn't know where he is, but reports do not list Daniel among any dead or in field hospitals. It will take time yet to find everyone who has gone missing. Even now Daniel could be on his way to you. Oh, Evie, I do hope he is! He has not sent word to his family, but I pray you do not take his silence as anything except a husband eager to get home to his wife. I pray to see you both again soon. I have missed you, dear sister.

My next news will no doubt shock you—I wish to visit you in Montana. Five years ago you left, and four of those burdened by war. It has been far too long, and I do hope you will not try to talk me out of coming. Will you consider Mother's request? She told me how much she longs to see you again, and I know Papa is of a similar mind. I explained to them both that surely you could not leave when Daniel must be on his way to you. Your letters these past years have painted your new home in such vivid wonder, and I long to see it for myself. I have not spoken to Mama or Papa of my plans. They will most certainly disapprove, yet I feel I must do this. I miss you, Evie.

Yes, it is decided. I was uncertain in my conviction to travel such a great distance. After all, you are the adventurer in the family, but now I am resolved in my plans. Please do not tell them. I promise I will speak with them soon, and I shall write to you of my arrival.

Be well and safe, Evie, and please do not fear. I feel in my soul that Daniel will return. Never have I known two people more destined to love for all time.

Your most devoted sister,
Abigail

TWO DAYS LATER and Evelyn still thought of her sister's letter. Abigail was the sensible and dutiful daughter, not prone to fanciful thoughts. And yet, she desired to leave home. Their parents would not allow their beloved young daughter to travel such a distance on her own, but who would they send with her? Abigail had been right about one thing—Evelyn had no plans to leave Montana, not when Daniel might still be alive.

She sat in the rocking chair on her front porch, enjoying the dance of clouds and sun over the mountain peaks. Snow still capped the highest of the mountains and the recent rains had brought a brilliant green to the valley. After an early morning in her gardens and her weekly visit to the general store, Evelyn considered new possibilities for the town. A few buildings remained empty, including the sheriff's office and medical clinic. The town wasn't large enough to warrant either on a regular basis, yet she felt strongly that both the position of sheriff and doctor should be filled.

She sat up and walked into the house. Her desk in the parlor faced the mountains and overlooked her gardens. The window stood open and Evelyn relished in the cool air and sweet fragrance of tall grass and freshly tilled soil. She picked up the handblown glass stylus her father had given her before she left home and dipped it into the ink well. She gathered her thoughts and set pen to paper, outlining the details of an advertisement for a doctor.

A few individuals in town knew enough to patch up injuries, but she wondered if a real doctor could have saved young William. Her inheritance was great, and the income from the timber and mining companies had only increased hers and Daniel's wealth. If she could not use the money to help the people entrusted in her care, what right did she have to it? Finding a doctor willing to live in a remote Montana valley might prove difficult, Evelyn thought.

She next penned an advertisement for a sheriff. Before she made copies and mailed them off to the nearest newspapers, and those as far off as St. Louis, she would approach Cooper about the position. Thus far he'd been willing to step in whenever the need for peacemaking arose, which wasn't often. Reluctant to accept a position that kept him in town, Cooper preferred to keep his freedom to roam and hunt when the mood suited him. Evelyn never mentioned to him that he rarely left town, always close by in case she needed him.

Their friendship deepened every year since Daniel had left. Evelyn once asked him why he did not go to fight, but he changed the subject without explanation. Despite what he wanted people to believe of him, she often wondered if there was more to Cooper than he allowed even her to see.

Thoughts of Cooper brought her mind back around to her husband. After three more weeks and too many nights crying herself to sleep, Evelyn began to lose faith that Daniel was alive. Abigail's contagious optimism had given Evelyn hope for a week, then two, but three? And still no word?

Harriett called out from the front garden. When Evelyn looked up, she moved her eyes to follow where Harriett pointed. She could not see the road and moved to the front door where she stepped outside.

"Harriett, what do you see?"

Harriett hurried around the side of the house and Tabitha stepped onto the porch beside Evelyn. Harriett said, "He's coming this way." She pointed and Evelyn's gaze followed. The sun shined into her eyes and she raised a hand to shield them. A lone man in dusty clothes with a beard grown too thick walked toward them. The road leading north of town led into the mountains. Those passing through traveled west or south to the mining camp looking for work.

Evelyn stepped out from beneath the protection of the covered porch, down one step then another. The man's gait was almost regal. He stood tall and straight, much taller than her. She peered closer trying to see his face. He stopped and a smile slowly formed on his face. He held open his arms, and Evelyn ran.

ALONE IN THEIR bedroom, the early morning light flitted across Daniel's face. She wept in his arms the night before, then loved him as she imagined doing for so long. His face was now clear of the thick beard and she gently touched a finger to the long puckered scar on his jaw. There'd been no words between them after he had bathed and ate. They relished in each other's presence, both realizing that soon enough the many words unspoken during their time apart would need to be said. Until then, they held one another, loved one another, and sank into sleep, in the comfort and security of one another.

A tear drifted down Evelyn's cheek to land on Daniel's face. She wiped the moisture away, surprised she hadn't felt them fill her eyes. Daniel opened his eyes and stared into hers. He lifted a hand to rest his palm against her damp skin. "I've waited and longed for this moment for four years. Can you ever forgive me?"

"Forgive what, Daniel?"

"I left."

Evelyn shook her head and pressed his hand closer. "I was never angry with you. I understood why you had to go."

"I don't deserve you, Evie, I never did, but God help me, I'll never leave you again." Their lips met and once again they lost their souls in each other. A few hours later, when they both awakened, the sun had reached higher in the sky and voices could be heard somewhere outside. No doubt news of Daniel's arrival had reached everyone. Many of them knew Daniel only as her husband, a man unknown. Others knew him briefly before his departure and called him friend.

They listened to the voices drift away, helped along by Tabitha and Harriett, both of whom Evelyn heard from where she guessed they stood on the porch, telling the others to leave the couple alone. Bless them, Evelyn thought.

"The town has grown some," Daniel said. "You've been busy. How's the timber?"

"It's a strong business, and we have the mine, too."

Daniel sat up and leaned back against the headboard. "A mine?"

"Yes." Evelyn nestled herself close to her husband while still facing him. "Do you remember Cooper, the guide who first brought us here?"

Daniel nodded.

"He found traces of gold in one of the river beds in '62. He swore there was gold to be found if we kept looking. He was right."

"Cooper found gold for you?"

"Not just for me, for the town. I financed everything and . . . told Cooper if we struck gold, he'd get forty percent of the mine. We did. He's given most of it back to the town, as have I. He insisted paying for the extra materials needed to shore up the mine to make it safer after a harsh winter. A sheriff's office and medical clinic were built, though I've only recently written advertisements for those positions."

Daniel's expression left Evelyn worried for a few seconds. "Are you upset?"

He covered her hands and drew her close. "No, my

dear. I have no right to be upset with anything you've done. Should you ever commit the gravest of sins I would still love and admire you. What you've accomplished . . . I should have been here."

"You're here now," she said, sinking against his bare chest. "You're here now and nothing else in this moment matters."

A few minutes of comfortable silence filled the air before Daniel said, "You and Cooper . . . have become friends."

Evelyn sat up, but remained close, her fingers entwined with his. "Good friends." She smiled and brushed the back of her hand over Daniel's chin. "He is as close to me as my sister, and just as dear."

Daniel smiled in return. "I sounded jealous."

"Perhaps a little. All I am and all I have has remained yours, and only yours."

Daniel hugged her close and pressed a kiss to the top of her head. "You haven't asked about what happened."

Evelyn had noticed the other scars. The one on his jaw must have bled terribly, but there were others she saw when he'd been in his bath, and a few her fingers touched on his back when they were in bed. He kept his life, his limbs, and his sanity. In her eyes, he was perfect.

"You'll tell me, when you're ready. I don't imagine the years are ones you want to relive anytime soon."

"Nothing in my previous life ever prepared me for what I witnessed on those battlefields. The fighting wasn't the worst part, though. It was the in-between. The quiet days and nights when we had only the cold and damp for company, and too much time to think of what we'd left behind."

Evelyn pressed her lips to his, held him close. "I will be right here, when you're ready, or if." She fidgeted with the sheet for a few seconds and said, "A few weeks ago I received a letter from Abigail. She said your name wasn't on any of the reports of dead or missing or hospitalized. Where were you?"

Daniel exhaled and closed his eyes briefly.

"I made a promise to someone, Evie. I gave him my word that if we both survived the war, I would help him find his family."

"I don't understand why—"

"I also promised him I wouldn't tell anyone, not even you, not until I was here and he was safe. Every day when I should have been traveling here, when I didn't write, I warred with my conscious, but I gave him my word."

"He must have been a very good man to be worthy of such a promise."

"Gordon Wells was his name. He was a slave, and he saved my life."

Tears once more filled Evelyn's eyes. She made no sound while she studied her husband's face. "Then he has my undying gratitude and devotion. Did he find his family?"

"He did. His son had died. He'd been traded away from the plantation where the family had slaved. His wife and daughter escaped six months before Lincoln's Emancipation Proclamation incited more escapes. Gordon lived in a loyal slave state, exempt from the proclamation. He thought if he stayed, his owner might not try to find Gordon's wife and daughter."

"Did it work?"

"For a time. His owner became ill and the overseer left. He made a deal with Gordon; he wouldn't send anyone after his family if Gordon remained until the end of the war."

"I don't understand."

"His owner was a desperate man by that time, having lost too many slaves."

"But Gordon—"

"Is honorable. He didn't try to explain his reasons for agreeing, and I didn't ask. I understood because in his situation, I would have done the same thing—to save you."

Evelyn brushed away a tear and leaned closer to her husband. "However did you two meet?"

"I was caught past Rebel lines on a scouting mission. I'd been shot near the plantation where Gordon lived. He found me in the river, pulled a bullet from my shoulder, and hid me until I was well enough to travel."

Evelyn touched the scar on Daniel's shoulder. "He sounds like a good man."

"I told him there would be a place for him, if he chose to come this far west."

Daniel had changed in the four years away. He'd always been a good man, a kind man, but Evelyn sensed in him a higher calling now. She believed herself untouched from the conflict, yet without her husband, she'd been forced to discover a side of herself previously unrealized.

Evelyn left the bed, slipped into her white linen robe, and walked to the window. Their bedroom faced the back of the house, away from prying eyes and open to a meadow and the mountains beyond. "It's this town, Daniel. Your dream, what you imagined this place could become, that's what kept me going. I felt you by my side every day. Even in this last week when I feared never seeing you again, I felt you in me. I'm not one for fanciful talk, yet I know this valley is blessed. We've endured much and we're stronger for it."

She turned back to him. "These mountains brought me comfort, this house, knowing it was ours, made me feel safe, and these people . . ." She returned to him. "The people gave me purpose. I thought of returning to Pennsylvania a few times, especially in those early days, but I couldn't leave them. I couldn't leave the home we'd built together."

Daniel pressed his forehead against hers, his arms wrapped around her. "And we'll continue to build. Whitcomb Springs may have started as my dream, but it became your legacy. I want to help you carry that legacy into the future."

Evelyn held his hands close to her lips, brushed a kiss against his warm skin. "The legacy is ours. Always and forever ours."

They talked and dreamed, shared hopes and plans, as they lay together with the mountain breeze brushing over them through the open window. Tabitha and Harriett left them alone, and though Evelyn wondered where they stayed, likely at the hotel, she didn't worry about them. From this moment on, adversity would have no power to defeat them. Trials and joy awaited in equal measure, yet Evelyn's heart overflowed with hope and wonder. When night descended and Daniel's stomach rumbled, Evelyn smiled and he chuckled. She said, "I'm a fair hand in the kitchen these days. It's time you were fed again."

"You've fed me well, with more love than I ever imagined. Are you ready for the next chapter of our story?"

"With you beside me, I am ready for anything." She grinned, a wildly happy grin that hinted at teasing. "Even if that *anything* includes Abigail. She has a notion to come to Montana."

Daniel leaned against the pillows, playing like a man in grave pain. "Heaven help us now."

Evelyn pulled a pillow out from under his head and hit him with it. Together they laughed and rolled in the tangle of sheets. Even though she believed somber days lay ahead as Daniel found his way back into the world, today their lives brimmed with only the glow from their combined joy.

THE END

Thank you for reading "Whitcomb Springs"! I hope you enjoyed the story; there's more to come.

Don't miss out on future books and stories in the Whitcomb Springs series:
www.mkmcclintock.com/newsletter.

A note from the author on the Whitcomb Spring series . . .

This is a collection of short stories, and the occasional novella, written by multiple authors. The series is filled with tales of adventure, danger, romance, and hope, and is set in the fictional town of Whitcomb Springs, Montana Territory. The stories span the years of 1865-1885.

Although each story may be set during a different time, they are stand-alone and may be read in any order. While the first stories will publish on March 15, 2018, this is an on-going project, so new stories may be published at any time by one of the participating authors.

"Whitcomb Springs" is the introduction to the series, set immediately following the end of the Civil War.

I hope you'll check out the other stories currently available in this series.
Visit: mkmcclintock.com/whitcomb-springs-series

Interested in reading more by MK McClintock?

The Historical Western Romance
Montana Gallagher series:
Gallagher's Pride
Gallagher's Hope
Gallagher's Choice
An Angel Called Gallagher
Journey to Hawk's Peak

Historical Western & Western Romance
Crooked Creek series:
"Emma of Crooked Creek"
"Hattie of Crooked Creek"
"Briley of Crooked Creek"
"Clara of Crooked Creek"

Historical Romantic Mystery
British Agent series:
Alaina Claiborne
Blackwood Crossing
Clayton's Honor

Enjoy her collection of heartwarming Christmas short stories any time of the year: *A Home for Christmas*

THE AUTHOR

AWARD-WINNING AUTHOR MK McClintock is devoted to giving her readers books laced with adventure, romance, and a touch of mystery. Her novels and short stories take you from the rugged mountains of Montana to the Victorian British Isles, all with good helpings of daring exploits and endearing love stories. She enjoys a peaceful life in the Rocky Mountains where she is writing her next book.

Learn more about MK by visiting her website and blog: www.mkmcclintock.com.